THE GRUNT AND THE GROUCH

Pick 'n' Mix!

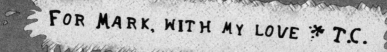
FOR MARK, WITH MY LOVE ✱ T.C.

STRIPES PUBLISHING
An imprint of Magi Publications
1 The Coda Centre, 189 Munster Road,
London SW6 6AW

A paperback original
First published in Great
Britain in 2010

ISBN: 978-1-84715-122-3

The right of Tracey Corderoy and Lee Wildish to
be identified as the author and illustrator of this work
respectively has been asserted by them in accordance
with the Copyright, Designs and Patents Act, 1988.

Text copyright © Tracey Corderoy, 2010
Illustrations copyright © Lee Wildish, 2010

A CIP catalogue record for
this book is available from
the British Library.

Printed and bound in the UK.

2 4 6 8 10 9 7 5 3 1

THE GRUNT AND THE GROUCH

GROUCH

Pick 'n' Mix!

TRACEY CORDEROY

ILLUSTRATED BY LEE WILDISH

Stripes

CONTENTS

1) PICK 'N' MIX!   7

2) SPICK AND SPAN!   37

3) RAT RACE!   69

CHAPTER ONE

Zzzzzzz… It was midnight. Everyone was fast asleep – well, not quite *everyone*.

A light was on in Crumbledown Cottage. Somebody was awake. Somebody was up and dressed. And that small green somebody was bursting with excitement.

"Grunty, wake up!" cried The Grouch, whacking The Grunt with his pillow. "Today's the day we're going to the cinema!"

"Ugh?" growled the big purple troll. "Who's that?" He opened one bleary eye. "Grouchy, *gerroff* – it's the middle of the night! Go back to bed, *trollbrain!*" He scratched his hairy bottom, gave a loud burp and closed his eye. "And don't wake me up until breakfast time – *or else…*"

Grouchy sighed and wandered back to his bed. He was much too excited to sleep. So he bounced up and down on his mattress instead, and thought about the film they were going to see…

It sounded *trollific!*

Everyone had been talking about it
for weeks. There'd been adverts in the
newspapers. Posters stuck up in town.
He'd read the words a hundred times…

Monster Plants!
Coming soon to a
cinema near you!

Well, now the film was here! And the cinema would be packed. Maybe they should start queuing *right now* or they might not get a seat.

Grouchy bounced off the bed and raced across the floor. He *had* to get Grunty up this minute!

"Breakfast!" he called. "Grub's up, Grunty!"

He pulled off a sock and wafted it under The Grunt's nose.

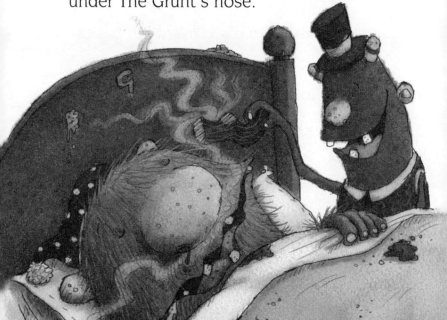

"It's yummy kippers and jam!" cried Grouchy. He popped the smelly sock back on and waited.

"Wha…!" snorted Grunty suddenly. His fat purple nose sniffed the air. *Mmmm* – something *did* smell good! Kippers and jam was his favourite.

"Race you down!" called The Grouch. He disappeared through the bedroom door before Grunty had time to check the clock.

"Oi!" yelled The Grunt, leaping out of bed. "Wait for me!"

He thundered downstairs and flung himself into a chair at the kitchen table. But wait…

"Hang on…" Grunty scratched his head. *Something* didn't look right.

Then, through the window, he noticed the sky. It was black and starry, with a big, shiny moon. It was still the middle of the night … he'd been *tricked*!

"Grouchy!" he bellowed. But The Grouch was now busy frying kippers.

"Get the jam out, Grunty!" he called, tipping them on to a plate. "Here – have my kippers, too! But please stay up. *Pleeeaaassse!*"

So The Grunt had breakfast in the middle of the night, but he flatly refused to start queuing for the film while the stars were out!

"Anyway, I've got *plans*." He winked. "I'll get us to the front of the queue whatever time we get there, don't worry!"

He stomped over to the goodies shelf to choose some tasty treats to munch at the cinema.

"Maggots? Earwax? Belly-button fluff? What will it be?" he cried. "Or how about … WE TAKE THE LOT!"

"*Trollific!*" cheered Grouchy.

CHAPTER TWO

After hours of waiting, it was finally time to go. The Grouch stood by the door, jiggling with excitement and clutching his jars of tasty treats.

"Come on, Grunty!" he cried. "The bus is coming."

"Keep your hair on!" yelled The Grunt, appearing with two jars of murky brown water. "I was just grabbing some drinks to take. And this pond water is *delicious*!"

They made the bus with seconds to spare and settled down on the back seat. But they'd hardly gone a mile when it pulled over and the driver threw them off.

"Hey, we're not even there yet!" growled The Grunt.

"Too bad!" yelled the driver. "Eating *maggots* on my bus! You're upsetting the passengers – listen…"

Loud retches and gurgly vomits could be heard inside.

The doors hissed shut and the bus drove off. "Miserable lot!" grumbled The Grunt. "Right, we'd better get walking!"

By the time they arrived at the cinema, the place was packed with peep-squeaks, all waiting for the doors to open.

Two people dressed as monster plants were entertaining the crowd by waving their leafy suckers about and making slurpy noises.

Grouchy hurried over to join in the fun. "My turn!" he cried. "I can slurp!"

"Not *you* again!" snapped a peep-squeak lady. "You were bad enough on the bus! Just *look* at my poor children."

She pointed at two titchy peep-
squeaks, both spattered in dried-up sick.

"Well, you can join the back of the
queue!" she said. "Go on!"

With that, her freckly peep-squeak
son pointed his monster-plant
zapper at Grouchy. "*Zap!*"

"Oi!" yelled The Grouch,
but suddenly Grunty came
thundering up.

"Come on, let's do what the lady says," he growled. But he smiled as he led The Grouch away. "Don't worry about her," he whispered. "We'll be at the front soon enough. I've got a queue-jumping plan, remember? Time for the windy-pop game!"

Five minutes later they were all set. Grouchy knew exactly what to do. He'd played the windy-pop game before. "OK," said The Grunt. "You go first."

Grouchy fished around in his pocket and pulled out a chunk of cheese. It was furry and smelled even worse than his sock! He nibbled a bit off the end, swallowed and waited.

After a couple of seconds there was a tiny **POP!**, followed by a faint whiff of mouldy cheese.

"Poo!" cried the peep-squeak man in front.

"Drains…" gasped his wife, holding her nose. "*Disgusting!*"

They shuffled forward a tiny bit, but stayed in the queue. Grouchy gave a sigh. He'd failed.

"Right, my turn!" said The Grunt, grabbing the chunk of cheese. He tossed it high into the air and swallowed it down whole. Then he jiggled about to get things moving and suddenly…

POP!

One-by-one, peep-squeaks started to gasp as a cheesy-maggoty-kippery pong (with a faint whiff of raspberry jam!) made its way steadily down the queue.

Everyone was doubled-up coughing as the cinema doors swished open.

"There!" cried Grunty, racing to the front of the queue.

First inside!

CHAPTER THREE

The trolls hurried in and found
themselves in a roped-off aisle leading to
a ticket kiosk. It had shiny glass windows
on three of its sides and behind it sat a
peep-squeak lady with narrow, frowny
eyes. "What's going on out there?" she
asked.

"Don't ask me!" shrugged The Grunt.
He nodded towards some big glass
doors. "Come on, Grouchy – through
there."

"Not so fast!" called the peep-squeak lady. "You need to buy tickets first! Right, how are you paying – credit card, cash or cheque?"

"What?" growled The Grunt. "But … we're *trolls!*"

"Mmmm…" sighed the lady. "So I see. But even *trolls* have to pay. So pay up or no film!"

The Grunt fished about in his pocket. The Grouch fished about in *his* pocket. Neither had credit cards, cash *or* cheques. Then Grouchy remembered their jars of treats – they could pay with something *much better…*

"'Ere you go – have this!" he beamed, flicking a big ball of belly-button fluff through the gap under her window.

22

Arraaggghhh!

The lady leaped off her stool.

"*Mouse!*" she screamed.

"That's not a mouse!" laughed The Grouch. "That's just..." But she'd already scurried out of a door behind her.

"Quick – now's our chance!" said Grunty. "Follow me!"

They hurried in through the glass doors and found themselves in the foyer.

23

There were screens showing clips of films. And popcorn stands selling popcorn. And a big, bright sign saying…

Grunty's eyes lit up. "That sounds good!" he cried.

They raced over, their jars of treats clanking as they went. But as they reached the kiosk, the attendant seemed to be leaving.

"Don't touch anything till I get back!" he said. Then he muttered something about a mouse and left.

The trolls could hardly believe their eyes. This place was *trollific*!

Shelves stacked with jars lined the walls, each one crammed with treats.

Wibble-Wobble Worms all squishy and
gooey, Choco-Mice with hairy tails,
Eyeball Gobstoppers with blood-red
veins, and lots, lots more…

"Right!" said The Grunt, unscrewing
the lid on the jar of maggots they'd
brought. "Let's do
what the sign says –
pick 'n' mix!"

With that, he
tipped the juicy
maggots into the
Wibble-Wobble
Worms and
gave them all a
nice mix around.

"There you go!" he said to The Grouch. "Beat that!"

So Grouchy picked a long, slimy bogey from his nose and dribbled it on to the gobstoppers. Then he mixed in a handful of belly-button fluff.

Ta-daaa! Beat that!

GRUNT AND THE GROUCH

As the trolls continued to pick 'n' mix, the place began to get busy.

"Oi, Grouchy!" said The Grunt, throwing him a bag. "Let's get some goodies before the best bits go!"

They filled two bags. Then, as they were leaving, the attendant came hurrying back. "Here!" beamed The Grouch, tossing him a sticky lump of earwax. "That pays for our sweeties! Keep the change!"

"What's *this*?" yelled the man. "Oi – come back!"

But the trolls were already racing off to get the best seats.

"Monster plants!" cried Grouchy. "Here we come!"

CHAPTER FOUR

"Let's sit at the front!" cried The Grouch, plonking himself down in a squashy chair. Grunty flumped into the seat next to him. They'd made it!

The cinema filled up quickly. The freckly peep-squeak boy from the bus sat down on Grouchy's other side. "*We've* got the best seats, *too*!" he bragged.

"Yeah!" scowled his sister.

"Not you two trolls *again*!" sniffed their mother.

THE GRUNT AND THE GROUCH

A few moments later, the lights
dimmed and excited gasps filled the air.
Everyone settled back in their seats, pick
'n' mix at the ready, and the film began.
Suddenly…

Gross!

There's a
bogey on my
gobstopper!

Maggots!

Urrrrgggh!

And on
mine!

"*Gross!*" cried the freckly boy. "There's a *maggot* in my sweets!"

"*Urrrrgggh!*" screamed his sister. "And in mine!"

"*Belly-button fluff!*" cried a voice.

"*Bogeys!*" screeched another. Then someone even started being sick!

The Grunt and The Grouch looked puzzled. After all the trouble they'd gone to making the pick 'n' mix *extra* tasty, all the peep-squeaks could do was moan. Ungrateful lot!

The trolls turned their attention to the film. Very soon the monster plants made their first appearance. They had pinchy claws and slurpy suckers that hoovered up whole buildings! Everyone hid their eyes in horror, whilst the trolls cheered and clapped. Wow – these monster plants were *trollific*!

But then the film got really sad when a peep-squeak invented a monster-plant zapper and started to zap the monster plants and turn them into *friendly flowers*!

"NO!" cried the trolls, as everyone started to whoop and cheer. Then the freckly boy next to Grouchy pointed *his* zapper at the screen.

"*Zap!*" he cried, pressing the trigger. "Gotcha!"

"No – give me that!" yelled The Grouch, wrenching it out of his hand.

"*Mum!*" wailed the boy at the top of his voice. "The little troll's getting me!"

Suddenly, a big beefy man with a badge saying "Manager" appeared. He turfed the trolls from their seats and marched them out into the foyer.

"Yes, that's them!" frowned the ticket lady waiting outside the door. "Set that killer mouse on me, they did!"

"And where's my money?" cried the pick 'n' mix attendant. "You don't pay for stuff with *earwax*! That's *disgusting*!"

The manager glared at the trolls. "Right, you two," he bellowed, "follow me!" He led them down a narrow corridor towards the back door.

"Just let us see the end of the film. *Pleeaassse!*" begged Grouchy.

But the manager wrenched open the
door and slung them both outside. "And
don't come back!" he yelled, as he
slammed it shut.

Grouchy sat down in the narrow lane
and gulped back a tear. "Grunty, why
didn't you *do* something?" he sniffed.

"But I did!" cried The Grunt,
and from under his waistcoat
he pulled out … two monster-
plant suits! "Borrowed
them off some pegs in
that corridor!
These are
our tickets
back
inside!" He
winked.

Five minutes later, two monster-troll plants tiptoed in through the back door.

"Right," whispered Grunty, as they crept back into the film, "just stay at the back and nobody will know it's us!"

But, Grouchy's eyes shot straight to the screen. A friendly flower was growing a sucker! It was turning into a monster plant again!

"Watch where you're going!" hissed The Grunt. But Grouchy's foot was already tangled up in Grunty's sucker.

The Grouch tried hard to steady himself, but it was no use…

"Aaarraaggh!" yelled the freckly boy, as Grouchy's suckers lurched towards him. "M-m-m-monster plants! They're coming for us – EVERYBODY RUN!"

34

Within seconds the cinema was empty, and the trolls sat back down in their seats to watch the end of the film.

"Fancy a bogey-gobstopper?" asked Grouchy cheerfully.

"Go on then." The Grunt smiled. "Monster-troll plants love bogey-gobstoppers!"

CHAPTER ONE

Flump! The Grunt flopped down in his grubby armchair and rested his feet on a stool. He'd been busy doing jobs all day. Now it was time to relax! He sniffed the steaming bowl of meatballs and lumpy custard sitting on his lap. *Yum!*

Grunty dipped his finger into the custard and slurped it noisily. He gave a satisfied burp as he gazed around the room and very nearly smiled, for everything looked just about perfect…

Green stuff dripped from the ceiling. Brown stuff splattered the walls. The windows were smudgy. The sofa was muddy. The floor was thick with dust. And there were filthy mugs everywhere, with furry "things" growing inside. Yes – he'd untidied up *so* well! But, as usual, he'd done it all by himself.

"Grouchy!" he bellowed. "Where are you? You've missed the untidying up again. Why do I always have to do *everything*?"

With that, he heard the toilet flush. This was the very last straw! How many times had he told The Grouch *never* to flush the toilet. Trolls just didn't *do* stuff like that!

The Grouch bounded into the room. "Oooh, meatballs and lumpy custard!" he cried. "*Yummy!* Can I have some?"

"No!" scowled The Grunt. "This is all mine! Treats are for trolls who *untidy up*, not spend all day on the toilet reading comics!"

"I wasn't *reading!*" The Grouch smiled. "I was just looking at the pictures! Go on – give us a meatball, *meaniepants!*"

He grabbed the bowl, but The Grunt
held on and tugged it back towards him.

"Meatball, meatball, meatball!"
chanted The Grouch.

"*Gerroff!*" growled The Grunt. The big
purple troll glared at his small green
friend. "*Toilet flusher!*" he snarled. "Let go
… *or else!*"

Suddenly The Grouch grabbed a
meatball and hurled it at The Grunt.
"Food fight!" He giggled.

An hour later they were *still* food fighting when suddenly someone knocked at the door. The trolls stared at each other in surprise. No one *ever* called on them.

"Scram!" growled The Grunt. "Or we'll have you for supper!"

He spun around and his beetle-black eyes glared at The Grouch. "Have you invited anyone round?"

"Nope!" said The Grouch. "But wait – I know – it must be Father Christmas! Ten months early! Cor – lucky us!"

"Don't be stupid!" growled The Grunt, as the knock sounded again. "Father Christmas doesn't knock. He uses the chimney, *trollbrain*!"

GRUNT AND THE GROUCH

The Grunt stomped over to the door to investigate, but he'd barely taken three steps when the letter box opened with a click and a pair of bright red lipsticky lips appeared on the other side.

"No!" gasped The Grunt. He stared at the lips in horror. "Anyone else…" he muttered, "…*but not her!*"

"Gerald, dear!" sang the lipsticky lips.

Great-Aunt Gretal knows you're there! Open the door... Don't make me count to three!

Chapter Two

"Gerald!" laughed The Grouch in a funny "lady" voice. "Gerald – is *that* your real name?" He threw himself down on the filthy floor in a fit of snorts and giggles.

"Gerald Grunt!" he chuckled. "Grunty Gerald!"

"So what if it is!" snapped The Grunt. "Stop mucking about and help me get rid of her!"

He sidled up to the door.

"Gerald's moved to, um … far away," he called back through the letter box in a funny voice. "So hop it! I mean – so – er … goodbye!"

The lipsticky lips at the letter box smiled. "Enough of this teasing!" they said. Then they started counting, "One … two … two-and-a-half…"

"OK, OK!" snapped The Grunt. "I'll open the stupid door!" He tugged it open, and there on the doormat stood his Great-Aunt Gretal!

The Grunt's great-aunt was the scariest troll The Grouch had ever seen. She was raspberry pink. And raspberry shaped. In fact, she looked like a monster raspberry with masses of curly green hair!

She had a huge purple handbag full of
revolting stuff. Grunty shuddered at the
thought of it. She had hankies in that
handbag which she'd try to make him use.
She had bubble bath and soap and
squirty perfume! She had combs and
spare combs and toothbrushes and *lists.*
Lists of cruel, nasty things she'd try and
make him do…

Like eat stuff with a knife and fork …
wash his smelly socks … scrub behind
his ears (and horns) and even *flush the
toilet*!

Great-Aunt Gretal waddled inside,
dragging an enormous suitcase. It looked
like she was hoping to stay. Well, he'd see
about that!

"Gerald!" she beamed, kissing The

Grunt with her big lipsticky lips. "And *look*!" she cried, smiling down at The Grouch. "Who's this little *cutie*?"

Grouchy gave a horrified gasp, then shot under the table. He didn't like the look of her at all!

"What a darling!" smiled Great-Aunt Gretal, peering down at him. "Though a bit of a wash wouldn't hurt."

Then she noticed the state of the house and her squashy pink nose wrinkled in disgust.

"*Goodness!*" she gasped. "It's a good job I'm not in any hurry." She opened her bag and fished out a can of rose petal polish and a duster. "Time we got this place shipshape, Gerald!"

"*Wait!*" cried The Grunt, looking

terrified. "Is that? Oh no – I'm allergic to roses … and petals … and *especially* to polish!"

"Oh, Gerald!" tutted Great-Aunt Gretal. "Don't be silly!"

Pssst! A whiff of roses blasted through the air and Grunty felt something hit his horns. He backed away, but her fluffy duster was there before he knew it. How *dare* she! He'd been *polished*!

"What's next?" she said, but Grunty wasn't hanging around a minute longer.

"Come on, Grouchy!" he cried, fishing The Grouch from the pile of pants he'd been hiding in under the table.

The Grunt turned to his great-aunt. "We're going upstairs!" he growled. "We need to do important stuff … by ourselves!"

"That's right!" sang the monster raspberry. "You go and tidy your room! And, when I've finished here, I'll cook us a nice healthy supper!"

CHAPTER THREE

Grouchy shut the bedroom door.

"Grunty!" he gasped. "Who *is* that
monster and what's she doing here?"

"She's my great-aunt," groaned
The Grunt, "but I dunno why she's here!
We need to think up a plan to get shot
of her!"

"Well, I hope we can…" sighed The
Grouch. "'Cos either *she* goes or *I* do."

So they sat and thought. Then sat and
bickered. Then just sat squeezing spots!

Suddenly, an idea popped into Grunty's head.

"I've got it!" he cried. "Operation Ghost Troll! Even *she* won't want to stay if the house is *haunted*!"

"H-h-haunted!" gulped Grouchy. "But I d-d-don't like g-g-ghosts! I'll have to leave too…"

"No!" cried Grunty. "The ghosts will be *us*!" He tugged the dirty sheets off the bed and shook off the toenail clippings. "These are for our costumes! Listen…"

Grunty explained that, later that night, when Great-Aunt Gretal was asleep, they'd dress up like ghosts, creep to her bedroom and tell her (in a ghosty voice) to hop it!

"Then," said The Grunt, "she'll scream and leg it."

"And we can go back to normal!" cheered Grouchy.

They settled down to make their costumes, imagining what fun they were going to have. When they'd finished, they tried them on and were just doing a spot of creeping and moaning when,

Gerald! Cutie! Supper!

"Coming!" the trolls called back. They pulled off their costumes, stuffed them under the bed, then hurried downstairs feeling very pleased with themselves – soon it would be time for Operation Ghost Troll!

Downstairs, a pongy, rosy smell hovered in the air. And there on the table sat supper … pea pie!

"Now, boys," said Great-Aunt Gretal, "I want to see your best table manners."

The trolls picked up their knives and forks, and started to eat. The food tasted horribly healthy. Then, suddenly, Grunty's meal "accidentally" ended up on the floor, and as Great-Aunt Gretal was cleaning it up, the trolls found a much better use for their forks…

Ping-pong-peas! Top game!

The Grouch aimed a pea at Grunty's nose and ducked when three came flying back.

"Boys!" called Great-Aunt Gretal. "Stop it at once! Bed, *now!*" The trolls hurried off upstairs. *No* dinner was better than pea pie!

Ten minutes later they were sitting in their ghost suits when they heard Great-Aunt Gretal thump up to bed. Soon her great snores shook the walls. It was time!

As they shuffled along the landing, Grouchy started giggling. "Can I tell her to hop it? *Pleeaaaaasssee!*" he begged.

"*Shhh!*" hissed Grunty. "She might hear! OK, but remember, *say it like a ghost!*"

The Grunt opened the bedroom door and they both tiptoed inside. It was dark in Great-Aunt Gretal's room. Very dark.

"Whooo**O**oooo!"

moaned The Grunt in a ghosty voice.

"Whoooo**OOOO**ooo**OOOO**ooo!"

moaned Grouchy too. "Hop it, you …
great big raspberry!"

They waited. Any minute now she
would scream and leg it…

But all was quiet.

Dark and quiet.

Then suddenly…

"*Whooooooooooo!*"

…something moaned back.

Then something big … and round …
and ghosty loomed towards them!

"Arrrgggh!" screamed the trolls,
legging it out of the door. "*G-G-G-G-
Ghhooosst!*"

When they'd gone, the big, round
ghost switched on the light…

CHAPTER FOUR

As the week rolled on, the trolls tried everything to get rid of Great-Aunt Gretal.

They hid plughole hair in her coffee, sneaked maggots into her bed and washed her bloomers in pongy pond water. But the tough old raspberry wasn't budging!

Then, early one morning, before Great-Aunt Gretal woke, the trolls were downstairs scoffing kippers and jam when…

"Wow!" smiled The Grouch. "I think I've just had an *idea*!"

"Ugh?" grunted Grunty. "*You* don't get ideas!"

"Well I did, just now!" beamed Grouchy. "It's a getting-rid-of-*her* one too!" And, even though Grunty looked a bit put out, The Grouch told him all about it.

"*What?*" boomed The Grunt when The Grouch had finished. "Keep the house clean! Have a bath! What do we want to do *that* for?"

"'Cos then she'll go!" Grouchy smiled. "'Cos she'll have nothing to do! See, she keeps on cleaning stuff, but we keep messing it up! So, if we keep things neat – just for once – *ta-daaaa*!"

"But…" spluttered Grunty. Then he stopped and thought. He couldn't believe it, but *maybe* … The Grouch was right.

"OK!" he growled. "But this had better work! Right – you use the bathroom first and…" (He took a deep breath.) "…don't forget to flush the toilet!"

That morning, when Great-Aunt Gretal came downstairs, a pot of tea (in a clean teapot), two neat triangles of toast and a jug of freshly picked flowers were waiting on the kitchen table.

"Oh!" sang Great-Aunt Gretal. "What a lovely surprise!"

Then she noticed *the trolls* were
spotless, too. Even Cutie had scrubbed
behind his horns! They were trying hard,
at last!

For the rest of the day, Great-Aunt
Gretal had very little to do. Grunty and
Grouchy kept the place neat, and waited
on her hand and hairy foot!

By breakfast time next morning, Great-Aunt Gretal's enormous suitcase and her huge purple handbag were sitting by the gleaming front door. They'd done it!

"Oh…" tutted Grunty. "You're leaving – so soon!"

"Yes! My work here is done. You boys have changed your ways!" said Great-Aunt Gretal proudly.

She picked up her suitcase and waddled out of the door. "Gerald – do keep Cutie clean!"

"I will!" said The Grunt, crossing his fingers behind his back.

Then he closed, locked and bolted the door. She'd gone!

To celebrate, Grunty picked his nose and flicked it at The Grouch. Then they flopped down in their spotless armchairs and tried to forget that she had ever been.

Eventually, Grunty stood up. "Oi, 'Cutie'!" he cried. "It's time we had a … *let's get grubby party!*"

Ten minutes later, the place looked just about perfect.

Green stuff dripped from the ceiling. Brown stuff splattered the walls. The windows were smudgy. The sofa was muddy. The floor was thick with dust.

Suddenly, there was a knock at the door. "WHAT?!" yelled The Grunt, as he stomped across to answer it. "Not *another* visit— aarrrrrgggh!" He tripped over something sitting by the door and landed on the floor. He got to his feet and stepped back in horror. It was something big … and purple … which smelled of roses!

Click! The letter box opened and two big lips appeared. Two big bright red lipsticky lips…

THE GRUNT AND THE GROUCH

"Gerald … Cutie!" they sang. "Great-Aunt Gretal's forgotten her handbag! Open the door! I know you're there…"

Don't make me count to three!

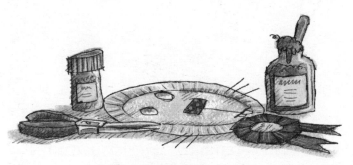

CHAPTER ONE

Gasp! The Grouch peered out of the window. "Grunty!" he cried. "There's a peep-squeak man by our gate. Look!"

"I'm busy!" scowled The Grunt. "Go and tell him to hop it!"

He squeezed a spot on the end of his nose and a stream of pus shot out. He grabbed a jar to catch it, but just missed.

"Bother!" he roared. He glared at The Grouch, but Grouchy beamed back, bursting with excitement.

"But Grunty!" he cried. "The peep-squeak looks like he's about to be sick."

"Sick?" said The Grunt, looking instantly less grumpy. The sick bag on their goodies shelf had been empty for ages. With Halloween coming up, a lovely pile of lumpy sick would be perfect for trick or treat.

"Right!" said The Grunt, snatching up the sick bag. "Follow me!"

They hurried outside. The peep-squeak man was still slumped by the gate.

"Oh dear!" said Grunty, trying to sound sorry. "You look *terrible*! Are you going to be sick?"

The peep-squeak man nodded. His face was almost green.

"Well, you've come to the right place!" The Grouch beamed. "We'll look after you."

They darted through the gate and ushered the man up the garden path. Grouchy held the sick bag in front of his face, just in case.

"In you go…" said The Grunt, guiding him through the front door. The man flumped into Grunty's chair and Grouchy popped the sick bag on his lap.

"So, did you have a nice big breakfast?" asked The Grunt.

"*Ugh…*" groaned the man. "Huge."

"Sausages?"

"Yes."

"Bacon?"

"Yes."

"A nice big greasy egg?"

The peep-squeak man nodded and clutched his tummy.

The trolls rubbed their hands together. *This* sick was going to be amazing! "Better out than in!" Grouchy beamed, pointing at the sick bag.

But suddenly the peep-squeak man staggered to his feet. "Got to go…" he groaned. "I'm a teacher at Sparkleton Primary. Have to get to school…"

He swallowed hard, rubbed his tummy and shuffled towards the door. "It's Class 3's award ceremony today – the RATS Awards. Only happens once a term. Parents come and Mr Spickspan makes a speech… I really *must* go…"

Grunty gasped. Had he heard right? Rats Awards sounded *amazing*!

He could see it now. Tons of rats –
probably class pets – all scurrying about,
competing for wonderful prizes!

There'd probably be a *Messiest Cage
Award* ... a *Best Biter Award* ... and a
*Fastest To Chomp Through The Rubbish
Award*. He and
Grouchy
couldn't
miss
this...

"Wait!"
cried The
Grunt,
steering the
man back
towards the
chair.

"Er … Mr … er … Smart…" said Grunty, noticing a badge on his jacket. "Think of your class! You can't go to school like that! You'll pass on all your lovely – I mean – *horrible* germs. We're teachers! *We'll* look after your class – won't we, Grouchy?"

"Uh?" said The Grouch. Grunty gave him a nudge. "Oh yeah – course we will! You just stay here, relax and be sick!"

The peep-squeak man gave a grateful smile and sat back down.

"Right, we'll be off then!" said The Grunt, racing to the door. "And when you finish being sick, leave the bag on my chair and shut the door behind you!"

CHAPTER TWO

In no time at all the trolls were at the school, peering through its freshly-painted gate into the playground. It was packed with titchy peep-squeaks waiting for the morning bell. But something just didn't look right…

Suddenly, they realized what that something was – everyone was neat and tidy! No runny noses. No scruffy hair. No giant holes in jumpers. Everyone and everything was spotless!

"Are you *sure* we've got the right school?" asked The Grouch.

"Yes!" snapped Grunty, opening the gate. "Come on, and let me do the talking!"

They were met in the playground by a tall thin man. His suit was stripy and his head was pointy. "Good morning," he said, inspecting the trolls. He gave a small cough, then frowned. "I'm Mr Spickspan, the head teacher. Can I help?"

"Look!" gasped a boy, staring up at The Grunt. "*Real monsters!*"

"Don't be silly, Fred!" said Mr Spickspan. "These are … er…"

"We're tr—teachers!" said Grunty. "And we've come to teach Mr Smart's class 'cos he's sick."

77

THE GRUNT AND THE GROUCH

"S-sick?" spluttered Mr Spickspan. "But my teachers are never sick! No one's *ever* ill at my school!"

It's spotless!

"Well, Mr Smart's sick today," growled The Grunt.

Mr Spickspan's left eye twitched nervously. These supply teachers were dreadfully scruffy, but they'd have to do. "Right then," he snapped. "Follow me!"

He led the trolls in through a door, then along a spotless corridor and into Mr Smart's classroom.

"Here…" he said, handing them a timetable. "Just make sure you follow this and I'm sure things will be fine." His left eye twitched again and he hurried off to ring the morning bell.

The Grunt sat down and put his feet up on Mr Smart's desk. He glanced at the timetable while he waited for the titchy peep-squeaks to come inside.

79

Tuesday

9am   Handwriting

9.30am   Silent Reading

10am   Playtime

10.20am   Spelling Test

11am   Mental Maths

Midday–1pm   Lunchtime
(No burping or slurping allowed!)

1.15pm   RATS Awards

3pm   Home time

"No…" groaned Grunty. "The Rats
Awards are *hours* away! What are we
meant to do until then? Everything else
looks dead boring!"

"I dunno…" said The Grouch. "Where
are the rats anyway?" They gazed around
the classroom, but there wasn't a single
rat cage in sight.

The titchy peep-squeaks walked in

silently and sat down in their places.
They stared wide-eyed at the trolls. They
didn't look (or *smell*) like teachers!
Nobody spoke as they took out their
handwriting books.

Grunty stood up and picked his
nose. "I'm Mr Grunt and he's Mr Grouch
and we're your new teachers," he said.
"Now tell me … where are you hiding all
the rats?"

Nobody spoke. Then a peep-squeak girl named Lottie slowly raised her hand. "But S-Sir," she said, "there are no rats. We d-don't have rats in this school."

"*No rats!*" bellowed Grunty. "But … this afternoon you've got Rats Awards! How are you meant to give them awards if there are *no rats*?"

"Sir," said Fred, "the awards are for us! RATS stands for Reading And Thinking Silently."

Grunty and Grouchy gaped at each other. They couldn't believe their ears! No rats … no piles of rubbish … no fun – just boring working in silence. *Unless…*

"Right!" cried Grunty. "Books away. I've got a much better idea…"

CHAPTER THREE

"This afternoon," said Grunty, "we're gonna have our own Rats Awards! But Rats Awards should be about these…" He drew a rat on the blackboard. "So what could you do to win an award, eh?"

Fred put up his hand. "I know!" he cried. "We could all make a rat's nest and the best one could win an award!"

"No – the *messiest* will win one of *my* awards!" said The Grunt.

Lottie put up her hand. "We could make a rats' assault course then all pretend to be rats. And the fastest one to get to the end would win an award!"

"Mmmm…" said Grunty. "Good idea … but we'd have to *look* like rats first, wouldn't we?"

"We could make rat masks!" beamed Grouchy. "And the meanest-looking one could win an award!"

"Well, what are you waiting for?" Grunty cried. "We've got *tons* to do before this afternoon! These Rats Awards are going to be *trollific*!"

He unlocked Mr Smart's cupboard and the children peered inside.

"Wow!" cried Fred excitedly.

There were stacks of neatly-folded tissue paper, unopened tubes of paint, brand-new balls of wool and a pile of paper plates perfect for making rat masks!

"Can I use glitter, Mr Grunt?" asked Lottie.

"Use whatever you like!" cried Grunty. "I am."

He rooted around in Mr Smart's drawer and found a rolled-up tie. It was grey – the perfect colour for a rat!

Quickly, he snatched up a pair of scissors and *snip, snip, snip* – cut the tie into little pieces! Then he glued the bits on to his mask, stuck on some pencils for whiskers and cut out two small eyeholes. There – he was done!

An hour later the class was teaming with rats of all shapes and sizes. Grunty surveyed his kingdom. "*Trollific!*" he said proudly.

As the bell rang for playtime, Grunty dived to open the door. "Out you go!" he cried. "But leave your masks here – you don't want to spoil the surprise for later. And don't forget to run!"

Outside in the playground, the other classes were all too scared to come near the new teachers, so the trolls and Class 3 had the climbing frame all to themselves.

"Let's splash in the puddles!" cried Grouchy, but Lottie shook her head.

"We're not allowed," she whispered.

"You are today," growled Grunty. "'Cos I'm on duty."

After that, Class 3 had the best playtime ever, leaping in puddles and playing "What's the time, Mr Grouch?". All the other classes stood by, gaping.

When The Grunt rang the bell, everyone walked in nicely. All except Class 3 … who *squelched*!

Before Grunty went back inside, he stopped off at the bins. Making rat's nests was their next job. The bins would have everything they needed! He opened a bin and peered inside. There was shredded-up paper, string, chewed straws, pongy milk cartons and all sorts! Class 3 would be spoiled for choice…

"Time to make rat's nests!" cried Grunty, heaving the bin into the classroom and emptying it on to the floor.

"Mine's gonna win!" cried Fred.

"No – *mine* is!" said his friend Billy.

"We all think you're *trollific*!" Lottie told the trolls.

By lunchtime, the classroom had never looked messier, but school had never been so much fun!

"Grub-time!" cried Grunty. "I hope it's nothing healthy."

"Last one to dinner…" giggled The Grouch, "…has to wash their hands!"

CHAPTER FOUR

Everyone raced into the dinner hall and up to the front of the queue…

"Oi!" cried Mrs Boil the cook. "Back you go!"

Quickly, The Grunt stepped forward and whispered in her ear. "What? Oh no!" she shrieked. She dashed away looking horrified, leaving the trolls to hand out the dinners instead.

"What did you say?" asked Grouchy.

"Not much." The Grunt sniffed. "Just

that I'd seen an army of rats in the corridor!"

The trolls dished out the dinners, mixing all the food together. Shepherd's pie tasted delicious swirled with strawberry mousse! The titchy peep-squeaks gobbled it up and had seconds.

Suddenly, Mrs Boil reappeared. She took one look at the state of the hall and turned an angry shade of red. "Quick," Grunty called to Class 3, "follow me!" He grabbed a bucket of leftovers and ran off as fast as he could.

"Why do we need leftovers?" asked Lottie.

"To make cakes to hand out at the Rats Awards!" Grouchy said excitedly.

"Leftovers cakes!" cried everyone. "Yummy!"

At ten past one, everything was ready for the Rats Awards. The children had spent the rest of lunchtime making leftovers cakes and turning their classroom into a rats' assault course.

Tables were now steep hills and slides. Chairs were bridges and tunnels. There was an ocean of rubbish to wade through. And swamps made from gluey paint. Everyone and everything was filthy!

At one fifteen precisely, the classroom door opened. "Welcome to Class 3's Awards for Reading And Thinking Silently!" they heard Mr Spickspan say from outside in the corridor. "Please do go in and take a seat."

A queue of spotless parents filed in. Their spotless mouths fell open. Their spotless children were … *rats*?!

"*Go!*" yelled Grunty, and an army of rats started scurrying about like crazy. What better way to kick things off than with the rats' assault course!

"*Stop!*" bellowed Mr Spickspan. But nobody could hear him. Class 3 were too busy having their best day ever!

"Would you like a leftovers cake?" asked Lottie Rat politely.

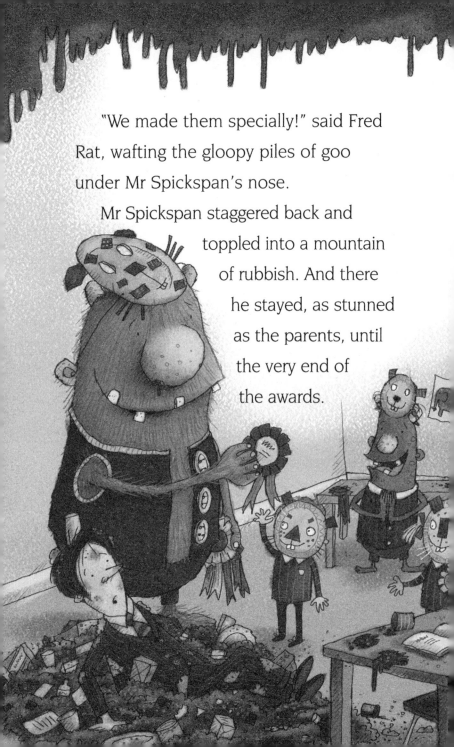

"We made them specially!" said Fred Rat, wafting the gloopy piles of goo under Mr Spickspan's nose.

Mr Spickspan staggered back and toppled into a mountain of rubbish. And there he stayed, as stunned as the parents, until the very end of the awards.

When Grunty had presented the final award to Billy for the meanest mask, he dug Mr Spickspan out. "Time to say goodbye," he growled at the head teacher.

"*Disgusting!*" hissed one parent.

"This school's gone to the dogs!" snapped another.

"No, to the *rats*!" corrected Grouchy.

Mr Spickspan wobbled to his feet. "I don't … feel … well…" he spluttered.

"Oh dear," said Grunty in his sorry voice. He winked at The Grouch.

"Here you go!" beamed Grouchy.